The BILLIONAIRE'S Christmas

The Billionaire's Christmas

CASSIE CROSS

Cover design by Mayhem Cover Creations
Interior formatted by

emtippettsbookdesigns.com

For the latest news on upcoming releases, please visit
CassieCross.com

CHAPTER *One*

Abby Kerrigan's life changed forever on the Monday before Christmas.

She'd been working herself ragged at her confectionery, *Sweet Talk,* making treats for the candy buying masses in Manhattan. It was her second holiday season in business, but the year prior had been less taxing because she had no name recognition and no customers. Her mother-in-law, Olivia, had been instrumental in getting her some key accounts, providing sweets for some high-class weddings and parties. After that, she got more business by word-of-mouth. While it was undeniably better than selling chocolates under a tent at the Union Square Market like she'd done when she was first starting out, she missed the freedom of making her own hours. Sure, she'd hired help and they were all wonderful, but she felt the pressure to succeed.

Her husband, Cole, had been as supportive as he could possibly be, going so far to tell her that it might be time for her to take a bit of a break and let her managers do all the managing for a while. Abby was convinced that no small part of that advice came from the fact that he was missing her just as much as she was missing him. Kerrigan Corp. was in the middle of a huge merger, which was keeping Cole at the office later and later every day, and more recently, required him to travel to London. He'd only been gone for a few days, and wasn't due back home until the day before Christmas Eve.

Abby had been feeling tired for weeks, but she powered through, pushing herself to the limit to make it through each day. But the nausea had started the week before last, and it wasn't letting up, so Abby booked a last-minute appointment with her primary care physician.

That afternoon, she walked into her doctor's office feeling ragged and run-down, hoping for a prescription and a miracle.

She walked out of her doctor's office feeling happier than ever, with a smile on her face and a card notating the date and time for her first sonogram clasped between her fingers.

A baby. She was going to have a *baby*.

Hands shaking, she picked up her phone to call Cole, but she froze when she saw his picture pop up in her contacts. She didn't want to deliver news like this over the phone when he was an ocean away. She wanted to tell him in person, where she could kiss him and hug him. Where she could see his smile and hold his hand.

He'd be home tomorrow evening; she could tell him then. Or maybe she could put the sonogram appointment card in a frame and wrap it up, then give it to him as a present. She couldn't help but smile when she thought of the adorably confused look he'd give her when he opened it up.

Yes, she decided. She'd wait, and surprise him on Christmas morning. What would be better to give him than something all of his money couldn't buy?

Sitting in the office of the flagship location of her candy store, *Sweet Talk,* Abby propped her tired feet up on her desk and watched as the store manager, Jayne, took stock of the holiday themed candies they hadn't sold by the close of business. Even a flurry of shoppers buying last-minute presents weren't able to clean her out of an obscene number of peppermint-flavored chocolates and homemade candy canes. Abby loved this time of year, and she *loved* Christmas. Seemed that affection had translated into a serious amount of overstock.

"I overestimated the number of New Yorkers who like minty chocolate by a *lot,*" she said with a sigh. She reached for a saltine from the half-eaten pack to her right, then brought the corner to her mouth and nibbled along the edges. The nausea was getting a little better, but being around tons of chocolate all day sometimes didn't help the situation.

Jayne grinned, then hung her apron on the rack behind

the break room door. "Nah, they're out there somewhere. Probably stuck in traffic on their way out of town."

"That's what they get for traveling on Christmas Eve," Abby said, opening a small bottle of water. "Gridlock without any minty goodness to get them through it."

"We should work that into our holiday advertising for next year."

"I knew there was a reason why I hired you."

"So," Jayne huffed. "What are we going to do with all this?" She motioned to the ten pristine white candy boxes that were perched on the long prep table on the opposite side of the room.

"Someone from the shelter over on Lafayette is going to be here to pick them up before eight." Abby looked at the clock and felt the keen sting of disappointment when she realized it was only seven. She'd been so worn-out lately, and it seemed like forever since she and Cole had a night just to themselves. She just wanted to go home to him, immediately if not sooner.

"You're not going to keep some to sell?"

"And do a half-priced sale? Nah." It wasn't like she needed the profit, and it would be a nice surprise for the people over at the shelter. "They'll do more good where they're going then they'll ever do here."

Jayne nodded. "Got any special plans for tomorrow?"

"Scott and Sara are spending the day with Sara's parents in Newport, and Cole's father was called away to Paris for business. His mom tagged along, so it's just the two of us," Abby said, absently rubbing her stomach. It finally seemed to be settled for the first time in hours. "I think we're just going to spend the day together at home." No plans, no hurry, no obligations. It was just what the two of them needed after the hectic rush they'd been in since Thanksgiving.

"It'll be the last quiet one for a while, huh?" Jayne said with a knowing smile.

Abby swallowed her response, choosing not to comment on that particular observation; Jayne had to know Abby was pregnant, but Abby couldn't bring herself to tell anyone before she told Cole. She had somehow managed to keep it from Becca even, and Abby had spoken to her at least three times since she had visited the doctor. No, she couldn't let it slip to Jayne, so Abby answered with a smile and a question of her own instead. "What about you? Got any plans?"

"Family dinner. Maximum drama, I'm sure."

"It'll be fine," Abby assured her with a laugh. "As far as I'm concerned, any family gathering that doesn't end in a fistfight or with someone calling the cops is a success."

That second, Abby's phone buzzed, skittering across her desktop.

Lonely without you. I sent a car over to pick you up.

Cole had returned home late the previous night, although he and Abby had managed to make love once before they both collapsed from exhaustion. She wanted to talk to him; to sit down and have a meaningful conversation with her husband. She missed his voice, and recognized how nice it was to know that he missed hers too. Abby grinned down at her phone, feeling this rush of love for him spread out through her body to her fingertips as she tapped out a response to his text.

See you soon. I love you.

Abby looked up from her phone, and Jayne gave her a soft smile.

"Why don't you go? I'll wait for the guy from the shelter and close up shop," Jayne said.

Abby slid her legs off the desk and took a gulp of water, considering Jayne's offer. She was hesitant to take it; since she'd been so exhausted lately, Jayne had been picking up a lot of the slack. Then again, that *was* what Abby paid her for, and was a main reason why Abby had included a handsome bonus in Jayne's last paycheck. Much as she loved her store, all she wanted was to be at home, in Cole's arms.

Abby stood and stretched, then walked over to the door that led to the store, glancing out the window to see the waiting town car.

"You're sure you don't mind?" Abby asked.

Jayne smiled as she shook her head. "Go."

Abby reached into the closet to her left and pulled out her coat, shrugging her shoulders as she slipped it on. "Merry Christmas, Jayne."

"Merry Christmas."

When Abby opened the front door to her and Cole's penthouse, she saw the light from their balcony beaming in through the glass-paneled French doors in their living room. He had a fire going and Christmas music playing softly in the background. The tree Cole had helped Abby decorate the day after Thanksgiving was lit up in the corner of the room, presents overflowing from beneath it.

"Cole?" she said as she started to shrug off her coat. It was then that some movement on their balcony caught her eye, and she recognized the outline of Cole's back as he looked up at the stars. Grinning, Abby buttoned up her coat and stepped outside. It was freezing, so she made her way over to her husband, whose consistently high body temperature made him feel like her own personal furnace.

If he was surprised by her presence, he didn't let on; he didn't so much as flinch when she wrapped her arms around his waist and pressed her cheek against his wool coat, right between his shoulder blades. He skimmed his palms over her sleeves until his hands covered hers.

"I've been waiting for you," he said. "I've missed you."

His voice was soft, barely perceptible in her position behind him, but she heard enough to make her smile.

"I've missed you," she replied as her husband twisted in her arms until she was tucked into his chest, his arms pulling her close. "Last night wasn't enough."

"Not nearly enough." Cole rested his chin against the

top of her head and pressed his nose into her hair, breathing deep. "You smell like mint." Abby could hear the smile in his voice as he ran his fingers through her hair. She'd missed this, just standing with him as he held her in his arms. It seemed like a lifetime since they'd just had a moment together to *breathe*.

"You smell like home," she replied as she gripped the lapels of his jacket between her fingers.

Cole slid his finger along the line of her jaw, then tipped her chin up until their lips met in a slow, tender kiss. Cole *felt* like home to Abby, too. When he pulled away from her, his eyes were as bright as his smile.

"Let's not do this again," he said.

"Do what?"

"The distance. Me going on business trips. I don't like it; I don't like being away from you."

"I don't like you being away from me," she admitted. That wasn't exactly news to Cole; whenever he went on business trips he always made sure to let her know just how much he'd miss her. He'd spend hours and hours telling her, with his lips pressed against her breasts, his head between her thighs, his body pressing into hers as he made love to her with abandon. Then he'd slide out of their bed, put on his three-piece suit and head off for another day as the leader of a multi-billion dollar conglomerate, and she'd head off to one of her stores, trying to make a name for herself in the gourmet world.

They were making it work; it wasn't like things between them were strained or anything - not even close, but she wanted him around more. She wanted to be around *him* more. Sometimes she found herself missing the days when she was still his assistant, all of the access she had to him then. During the long nights she sometimes spent at the shop, she missed being able to walk right into his office and see his smile, to be able to talk to him whenever she wanted to. Of course, she romanticized those days and the missed opportunity of them, because she and Cole hadn't even been dating. She could imagine how much better her work life would've been sometimes if they had been.

Cole snuggled her closer to his body, trailing his lips across her forehead. "Tonight, I'm going to show you just how much I missed you."

Abby felt her heart skip a beat, and looked up at Cole with fire in her eyes. She loved it when he showed her things; it was one of his many considerable talents. "Oh yeah?"

Cole nodded slowly. "Yeah."

It was unfortunate that her stomach took that opportunity to growl rather loudly, making Cole laugh.

"I guess we better take care of that first, huh? You're gonna need some stamina."

"Lots and lots of stamina," Abby replied. "Hours of it."

CHAPTER *Two*

"I ordered Chinese," Cole told Abby as they swayed together, dancing to some silent rhythm as they stood together on their balcony.

"My hero," she teased. "You always seem to know just what I need right when I need it."

Cole sighed and pulled her against his chest. It was freezing outside, and the air even *smelled* cold. He was hoping that it would snow overnight; ever since the weather man mentioned the possibility of a white Christmas, Abby mentioned it every chance she got. Cole had to admit that he was looking forward to spending the day alone with her, just the two of them curled up together in front of the fireplace. He couldn't wait to surprise her with the gift he'd bought for her. He'd gotten her a few things she'd been wanting, but the big surprise was a two week-long trip to a high-end spa in

Fiji. He knew she was tired, and they could both use a break from their high-demand jobs.

"I thought taking care of you was part of that whole for-better-or-for-worse thing we agreed to when we got married," he said, smiling.

"I don't think being thoughtful and intuitive are necessarily part of that bargain, but words cannot express how glad I am that you're both of those things."

"And more." Cole playfully nudged her to let her know he was teasing.

"And so much more."

He would never get tired of knowing how much she appreciated him. In a marriage where he felt like he got the better end of the bargain, it was nice to know that he wasn't always the only one who felt that way.

Cole pressed his lips to Abby's forehead just as their doorbell rang. He reluctantly released his wife, then took her hand and led her inside.

"I'll get the plates out," she said as she headed to the kitchen.

Cole greeted the bellman at the door; he'd brought their food up from the lobby. He slipped the elder gentleman a generous tip and wished him a Merry Christmas before closing the door and heading back inside. He found Abby in the kitchen, sitting in front of one of two place settings she arranged on the far side of the island.

"What did you get?" she asked, sounding so eager that if he didn't know better, he'd think she hadn't eaten in days. He had to laugh at her enthusiasm.

"Beef with broccoli," he said as he pulled the container out and placed it on the counter. "Cashew chicken, lo mien, and that wonton soup you love."

"Ooooh, gimme," Abby said, reaching out for the soup.

Cole handed it to her as he opened the beef with broccoli, and he heard the container's plastic top hit the granite countertop, accompanied by a stomach-turning retch. He watched, completely stunned, as his wife covered her mouth with her hand and ran out of the room with him hot on her heels.

Cole absentmindedly moved the sponge back and forth over the granite countertop, not really cleaning, not really thinking about what it was he was doing. His thoughts were in the other room, with his sick wife. He had tried to follow Abby into the bathroom, but she asked him to give her a minute, and when she heard him pacing outside the door, she begged for a few minutes more. Not one to deny his wife anything she needed, Cole busied himself in the kitchen. He tossed their food down the garbage disposal, then walked the containers to the trash chute down the hallway. He opened the windows, turned on a fan, lit a few candles, and sprayed nearly every surface of their kitchen to get rid of the smell.

Opening the windows had helped, although it quickly lowered the temperature in their penthouse a few degrees. The air smelled like snow, and Cole found himself closing the windows, knowing that the last thing Abby needed was a chill if she was getting sick. Cole wondered if there was a virus going around; his assistant had been sick earlier in the week. Could he have brought something home with him that had made Abby ill?

Cole looked up at the clock on the wall by the pantry. It had been five minutes since he knocked, and he hadn't heard Abby come out. She'd asked him for time, and he'd given her enough of that, right? Wouldn't hurt to just walk over to the door and give it a little knock.

"Abby?" he called softly. "Are you okay?" Through the thick wooden door, he could hear the gentle rhythm of her brushing her teeth.

"I'm fine," she mumbled around what he was sure was a mouthful of toothpaste. Just the sound of her voice made him smile. He heard the water running, and the next thing he knew the door was opening. In the bright light of the hallway, Cole looked at her, really *looked* at her for the first time in what felt like weeks. He knew she'd been tired, but the dark circles under her eyes made her look absolutely exhausted. Her skin had a pallor to it that he hadn't ever seen on her, and he was hoping it was just the aftermath of her being sick. He reached out for her, slid his hands across the curve of her shoulders and along her neck until he was cupping her cheeks.

"You're not fine," he whispered, and he could hear the worry in his voice even though he was trying desperately to tamp it down. "You've been running yourself ragged, and I've been too damn busy to notice. Not anymore," he said, gently pulling her toward their bedroom. "You need to lie down."

"Cole," she said, and if he didn't know any better, he could almost hear a hint of amusement in her voice.

"I'm going to go and get you some water, and then I'm-"

"Cole."

"-going to call Doctor Prader to see if she'll make a house call tonight. If not, I'll find someone who will. Surely there's-"

"*Cole*," Abby said tenderly but emphatically. She tugged on Cole's hand, and he stopped and turned to face her. She was smiling softly, and it made her look like her illness was a distant memory. She pressed her palms against his cheeks, gently cupping his face. "I'm not sick."

Cole's brows furrowed in confusion. "You're sick, I saw you get sick, you…" He thought better of telling her that she looked sick; regardless of how she was feeling, he knew that voicing that particular thought wasn't going to have a good outcome for him.

Abby shook her head, grinning. Even though he was incredibly confused, that smile calmed him; it made his heartbeat slow down to an even pace, and it soothed his nerves.

"I'm not sick. I've already seen a doctor."

Cole reached out and put his hands on her waist, because he just needed to touch her. "You…what?"

Abby skimmed the pads of her thumbs across Cole's cheekbones. "I was going to tell you tomorrow. I thought…I don't know, I thought it would be a nice surprise. I found out three days ago, but you were still in London, and by that time it was so close to Christmas that I thought maybe it could wait, and now I'm realizing that wasn't such a good idea, because I can't hide the barfing. It's been happening with greater frequency lately, and yeah…not such a great idea on my part."

"It's been happening with greater frequency?" he asked, and the only thing that was holding off the growing panic was that he got the distinct impression that he was failing to put the right puzzle pieces together and was missing something very important.

Abby laughed at him, and he couldn't help but think that it was the most beautiful sound he had ever heard. Then she pushed herself up onto the tips of her toes, and she pressed her lips to his. When she pulled back, she caressed his cheek, and he closed his eyes and leaned into her touch.

"Look at me," she said as she held him close, their noses brushing together.

When Cole opened his eyes, Abby's were wide and bright and happy. "We're going to have a baby."

Cole had prepared himself for the worst possible news, had braced himself to hear something terrible. So the lightness in Abby's face combined with the happy way she said said the words made it difficult for his brain to process them. He shook his head, eyes wide, like he was trying to shake himself out of a daze.

"What?" he asked, just to make sure he'd heard her correctly. It was the most obvious answer, he was surprised it took him so long to get it.

Abby had an endless amount of patience when it came to waiting for him to catch up with her, and this was no different.

"Were going to have a baby."

Cole couldn't help the sweeping sensation that rose up from his stomach and out to the far reaches of his limbs. A baby. They were going to have a baby. A laugh bubbled up out of his throat at the same time that his eyes became blurry with happy tears. God, they were going to have *a baby*.

"A baby?" he asked, like he just had to say the words to make them true.

Abby nodded, smiling.

"I love you," Cole said with this overwhelming joy that couldn't help but reach out its fingers and wrap itself around every single part of him. He couldn't find words to express all the hope and love and happiness he was feeling, so he pulled her into a soft, slow, tender kiss.

"I love you, too."

Cole slid his hand across Abby's belly, smiling all the while. "When?"

"July."

July. July didn't seem like nearly enough time. They had to get a crib and a stroller, and what else would they need for the baby? The fact that he didn't know made a tiny bit of panic burst through the joy. He had a niece and nephew, he should know these things. Burp cloths, they needed that. Pacifiers, bottles. He'd have to do some research on the internet once Abby went to sleep.

"Hey," Abby said softly, giving him a look full of such love that it made his knees feel weak. "We've got time, don't panic."

"There's so much to do."

"And we have months to do it. We'll be fine, Cole," she said soothingly. "For now, I was kind of hoping you would do something for me."

He swallowed back the knot of emotion in his throat and he nodded, gripping her hips, letting his thumbs gently graze her skin beneath her shirt. "Anything," he told her. "I would do anything for you."

"Make me a grilled cheese sandwich?" she asked sheepishly.

Cole laughed, then twined his fingers together with hers. "C'mon. I'll make you the best grilled cheese sandwich you've ever had."

"With tomatoes?"

"Yeah," he laughed. "All the tomatoes you want."

Cole sat across from Abby at the kitchen island and watched her happily munch away on her grilled cheese. He felt this overwhelming sense of protectiveness rising up in his chest at the sight of her, and something akin to pride at the way she was enjoying the sandwich he made for her. He couldn't take his eyes off of her, couldn't wrap his mind around the fact that she was carrying their child. He just wanted to wrap her up in his arms and keep her there for the next seven months. Not that he was going to become one of those overprotective, nervous husbands or fathers, but he just wanted to be there for everything. He didn't want to miss a single second of what was coming.

When Abby had finished her sandwich, she slid off her chair and walked over to the sink, then turned on the faucet and started to rinse off her plate.

"Leave the dishes," Cole said as he walked up behind her, pressing his lips against the back of her neck. Sometimes, after she'd spent a long day at the shop, her skin tasted kind of sweet, like there was a fine dusting of sugar all over her. Tonight was no different. Cole wrapped his arms around her waist, his palms gently resting against her belly as he pulled her back into the safe confines of his embrace. "I'll do them tomorrow."

Abby slid her hands along Cole's forearms until they were resting on top of his. They'd been together for so long now, but just the lightest hint of her skin against his had the power to give him goosebumps.

"An hour ago we didn't have enough time for everything we needed to do, and now you're procrastinating. What's it gonna be?"

Cole could hear the lightness in Abby's tone. The way her voice tilted up at the end of some of her words when she was teasing him was one of his favorite sounds in the world. Cole reached over her shoulder and shut off the faucet, then turned her in his arms, handed her a towel to dry off her hands, and cupped her cheeks.

"It's gonna be me making sure that all the things that have been keeping us apart from each other get pushed into the background, okay? Before we got married, I promised you I'd be there for the soccer games and the recitals and all of the important moments, didn't I?" He knew that Abby hadn't forgotten that promise; it had been so important to her then. But he wanted—no, he *needed*—to remind her that he hadn't forgotten about it either.

"You did."

"The important moments are now, Abby. I don't want to miss a single moment of this, okay? The dishes can wait, all this…insignificant stuff can wait. Work and all that…we'll figure it out. You and our baby come first; I don't want to spend my life chasing after professional success and missing the things that really matter. I just want to focus on us tonight," Cole said, looking down at her belly, hoping Abby could feel how true his words were, how much love he had for her and their baby.

"What exactly are you going to be focusing on?" she asked, not even trying to pretend that she wasn't flirting with him.

Cole gave her a look with a wicked gleam in his eyes as he took a small step forward, erasing whatever small amount of space was still between them.

"I'm going to focus on kissing you," he said, before he did just that. He could feel the goosebumps on her skin as he trailed his lips all the way down her neck to her collarbone. She melted into him like she always did, her arms wrapping around his neck as she leaned against his chest. "I"m going to focus on the way you get all loose when I touch you here." He slid his hand along the side of her hip, letting his fingers brush the skin underneath the waistline of her pants. Then they traveled towards her belly, and just below. "The way your breathing picks up when I part your legs and lick you here." His hand slid down, beneath her panties, until he was cupping her right where he knew she wanted him most.

Abby moved quickly, almost surprising him when she hopped up, using him as leverage to wrap her legs around his waist. Cole cupped her ass, cradling her body against his, and she let out a gasp when he turned her away from the counter.

"Where are we going?" she asked.

Cole knew she loved it when he'd take her quickly, all impulse and physicality, not even worried about finding a bed. There would still be time for that, but tonight was not that night.

"The bedroom," Cole replied, his voice gruff.

"But-"

He silenced her with a kiss, then pulled back and gave her a soft, sweet grin. "I just want someplace soft where I can take my time, okay?"

Abby nodded and closed her eyes. If her reaction was any indication, that was more than okay.

"What are you doing?" Cole asked as Abby slid his underwear down his hips. It was a stupid question, really, Cole knew *what* she was doing, he just didn't know why she was doing it. Tonight was all about giving *her* pleasure, about making *her* feel worshiped.

"So help me," she said as she trailed hot, wet kisses down his belly. "If you say something about how tonight is all about me, you're not getting another blow job for a month."

He laughed and relaxed his tense muscles, allowing himself to enjoy the sight of his wife on her knees in front of him, intent on providing him with whatever pleasure she could. "Okay," he said, sliding his fingers through her hair, tenderly caressing her scalp.

"I knew that would work. Relax."

"I am relaxed," he said, giving her what he was positive was a dopey smile.

"I just want to make you feel good."

"You make me feel good," he said. And she was making him feel so, so good. Just the simple, soft feeling of her lips and tongue on his skin left his cock rock hard and throbbing, aching for her touch. And Abby knew his body so well that she immediately gave him what he wanted, sliding her hand along his shaft in long, firm pulls with one hand as she gently tugged on his balls with the other. "Your mouth. I want your mouth."

Abby didn't oblige him right away, still stroking him and driving him higher and higher, to the point where he was ready to beg her to let him feel her mouth around him.

"Please," he ground out through gritted teeth, digging his fingers into the sheets until they were crumpled up between his fingers. "Abby, please."

She looked up at him, and all Cole wanted to do was kiss that wicked grin off her face. Then she flicked her tongue across the underside of the head of his cock, and he wanted that beautiful, warm mouth to keep up its current occupation. She worked him the way she knew he liked, taking him deep until he hit the back of her throat, making him groan and curl his toes as she swallowed and hummed around him. He tangled her hair through his fingers, pushing it aside so he could get a better look at her as she brought him to the edge of pleasure, made every single nerve on his body stand on end. Just when he had nearly reached the breaking point, Cole gently pulled Abby up so he could kiss her, and when he deepened the kiss he could taste himself on her tongue.

He lifted Abby up into his arms, then set her down on the bed, kneeling down in front of her in the place she'd just vacated. Cole kissed the insides of each of her knees, then spread her legs wide before he gripped her hips and brought her body right down to the edge of the bed.

"But I was just getting started," she said, her voice all low and sexy.

"So am I," Cole replied, brushing his lips along the inside of her left thigh. "So am I."

CHAPTER *Three*

If someone asked Abby to list her ten favorite feelings in the world, the gentle scratch of Cole's stubble against the inside of her thighs would most definitely make the cut. As would the slick slide of his tongue across her clit as he teased her, and the way his breath puffed against her wet skin when he laughed at the noise she'd just made, which was somewhere between a sigh and a moan. Whatever it was, Abby knew that Cole was intimately familiar with that noise, knew that she wanted more of whatever it was he was doing when she was making it.

This particular time he was torturing her by alternating licking and sucking, teasing her with the tips of his fingers, making her beg for more, *more* before he slid them inside of her, curling them up until they hit that perfect spot inside her as he worked her clit relentlessly with his tongue. She was teetering right on the edge of her orgasm, the muscles in her legs and abdomen clenching as she chased her pleasure along the tip of Cole's tongue. His arms were hooked around her thighs, giving her great leverage to grind against him, which was fantastic because he hadn't shaved in a couple of days and his whiskers were definitely doing interesting things.

"Is that good?" Cole asked.

"Yeah," Abby somehow managed to reply, even though it took everything in her to make her mouth work. "It's… yeah, it's good."

Then she ran her fingers through his hair, tugging on it the way he liked, and their eyes met. She couldn't see his mouth—he was still doing wonderful, *magical* things with it—but she could feel his smile against her, and that was enough to send her crashing over the edge, bucking her hips up off of the bed as Cole kept on, giving her time to ride out the waves of pleasure. Then she fell back against the bed, relaxed in a way that she hadn't been for so long, all boneless and light, breathless and happy.

"C'mere," she said, crooking her finger towards Cole.

He crawled up her body, peppering kisses along her hipbone, across her soon-to-be-swollen belly, up her ribcage and around her breasts, taking care not to be too rough, since she'd told him earlier that they were tender. Then Abby slid her hand along the back of Cole's neck and bought his lips to hers. The kiss was rough and needy, Abby sucking on Cole's bottom lip which was still wet from her, teeth nipping and tongues caressing.

Abby took advantage of the fact that Cole was distracted,

and reached down between them to stroke his dick, swirling the pad of her thumb around the moisture beaded at the tip.

"Abby," he warned, his voice almost a growl as her name found its way through his clenched teeth.

Abby kissed her way up the side of Cole's face, along his stubbly sideburns, until her lips reached his ear. "I'm not teasing you. I just want you, okay? Right now."

Abby wrapped her legs around Cole's waist, and she could feel him hard and ready right where she wanted him most. And just when she thought he was going to give her what she wanted, he slid his hand along the small of her back and pulled her up with him until he was kneeling on the bed and she was resting against the tops of his thighs. Cole kissed her, then slid his fingertips along her upper arms and down to her wrists where he clasped them in his hands and brought them up behind the back of his neck.

"Hold onto me," he told her.

She did exactly as he asked.

Cole cupped Abby's ass, then slid his hands down the backs of her thighs and lower, locking her ankles behind his waist as he sat down on the bed cross-legged. Their bodies were touching in every possible place, except the one place she wanted him most.

"Cole," she cried, shifting her hips. She wanted to sink down onto him, but she wasn't at quite the right angle. She needed his help.

He reached down and slid the tip of his dick along her wet slit, and Abby gasped when she felt him move along one side of her clit and then back down the other. Her heart was hammering in her chest. Cole's was too; she could feel the steady thump against her breasts. Abby shifted so she had a bit of a height advantage over him, and he took that opportunity to pepper kisses down the length of her neck and along her collarbone, taking time to suck on the skin at the crook of her neck.

"Please," she said, feeling desperate for him. "*Please*."

Her second plea must have broken his resolve, because he placed one hand on her hip to steady her as he used the other to push inside of her. Abby took a second just to feel him, squeezing him a bit the way she knew he liked. Cole grunted and sighed, overwhelmed, and rested his forehead against hers. Then Cole captured her lips and guided her movements as Abby rode him, resting her hands on his knees and leaning back so he could take in the view.

"You're so beautiful," he said, his voice kind of ragged. "Do you have any idea how beautiful you are?"

The sides of Cole's thumbs were gliding along the sides of her belly, and she never felt more beautiful than when she got to be with him like this: skin to skin, with nothing between them, his eyes full of lust and love and all the things there weren't enough words to express. Abby didn't know how to answer him, so she took his face in her hands and kissed him, long and slow and deep as they moved together.

Before long, Cole lowered her onto her back and propped himself up on his elbow above her, twining their fingers together. He fit perfectly into the cradle of her hips, and moved with slow, hard thrusts. Abby took his free hand and brought it to her lips, kissing each one of his fingertips.

"I love you so much, Cole," Abby whispered. "I hope you know how much."

He lowered his forehead to hers, until their lips were touching. "I do. I know."

Abby spread her legs further and moved them back toward her chest, allowing Cole to enter her at the perfect angle. And it felt so good—him moving inside of her—that any words that were on the tip of her tongue just flew away as Cole pounded into her, pushing her closer and closer to climax. Abby knew he was close too; his movements were getting more and more erratic, and she could see the way the pleasure was softening his eyes. Her orgasm hit her at once and she cried out, arching her back as she rode out the waves, her muscles fluttering around Cole. He followed her soon after, emptying himself inside of her as he tucked his head into the crook of Abby's neck, kissing her skin.

After, they lay together in their quiet bedroom, with Abby's head resting on Cole's shoulder as she closed her eyes, breathed him in, and tried to sleep.

Abby never slept better than when she was wrapped up in Cole's arms. Whenever he was out of town, Abby wasn't ashamed to admit that she'd take one of his dress shirts and button it around one of his pillows so she could still smell him while she was trying to sleep. Once Cole found out, he'd teased her about it, but it was done with love, and he made it a point to leave one of his shirts behind on the bed.

Tonight, even though Cole's arms were definitely wrapped around her (he was the big spoon, she was the little, and his left hand was splayed out protectively over her belly), she was unable to sleep. She had to admit though that insomnia due to happiness was probably one of the best reasons to be lying awake in the middle of the night. Her mind was buzzing; it was absolutely impossible to turn it off. She couldn't stop thinking about the fact that there was a *life* inside of her; a person that she and Cole had made. Which parts of the baby would be Abby, and which parts would be Cole? Would the baby have Cole's business sense? Would the baby have Abby's ability to see the good in people? Would the baby be healthy?

God, there was so much to do. What kind of crib should they get. Which stroller was the safest? Would she be able to breast feed? What color should they paint the nursery - would Cole even want to know what sex the baby is? Would she?

Abby's mind was going a mile a minute when she felt Cole shift behind her, tucking his knees behind hers as he pressed gentle kisses to the back of her neck.

"You need to give that beautiful brain of yours a rest," he said, then planted a kiss on the top of her head.

"I can't," she replied, twining her fingers through his. "I'm too excited to sleep."

Cole huffed out a laugh, and Abby could feel his warm breath fan across her shoulders. "That I understand."

"You too?"

"Definitely me too. What are you thinking about?"

Abby's fingertips trailed up and down Cole's arms as he pulled her tightly against his chest. "I'm wondering if you would want to know if it's a boy or a girl, or if you'd want to be surprised."

Cole tucked his chin against Abby's shoulder, and she knew he was running through the pros and cons of both knowing and not knowing. "I think I'd want to be surprised. We get so few good surprises like that in life, you know? We can pick out a girl's name and pick out a boy's name, and be ready either way."

Abby nodded, contemplating Cole's answer. "Does it matter to you?"

"What, if it's a boy or a girl?"

"Yeah. Do you have a preference?"

"My preference his healthy," Cole said. "I know that's the typical thing parents say, and I always thought it was kind of a cop out answer, but now that I'm in the position of having to give that answer, I really don't care. All I want is a healthy baby. What about you?"

Abby nodded. "Same."

Cole's hand moved across her belly, and Abby smiled.

"When will I be able to feel it?" he asked.

Abby had to laugh. "Feel it kick?"

"No, just *feel* it. See it. The baby, I mean. We probably shouldn't call it *it*. "

"I'm not really sure, but from what I can tell it might be a little while. We can ask the doctor at my sonogram appointment. Why the rush? In a hurry to let everyone know you're a manly man?" Abby teased.

"No," Cole replied softly. "It'll just make things more real. For *me.* It's *real* for me, but everything's happening in your body. I don't know what I'm trying to say."

Abby turned in her husband's arms, feeling a flutter in her chest about how flustered and unsure some parts of fatherhood were making him. Abby cupped his cheek, and Cole leaned into her touch. Then he slid his fingers through her hair and tilted her head up so he could press a kiss to her lips.

"I know what you're trying to say. This is *real* to me now, because it's my body and I can feel it. It'll be real to you when you can feel it. When you can see it."

"It's more surreal to me at the moment," Cole replied, kissing Abby's knuckles.

"You'll probably be wishing you hadn't wanted that realness when I reach the pickles and ice cream phase."

"But there's a super horny phase too though, right?"

Abby laugh. "Pretty sure there is, although I don't think we're there yet."

"You'll let me know when you are?" Cole replied, and Abby could see the mischievous glint in his eyes even in the darkness of their bedroom.

"Oh, I think you'll be the first to find out that particular bit of information."

"I better be," he said, trailing the tip of his index finger along the curve of her collarbone. "It's after midnight, so it's technically Christmas. Since we're up, want to open presents?"

Abby yawned, feeling her already present exhaustion start to pull on the edges of her consciousness. She was pretty certain that if she just closed her eyes she'd fall right asleep, now that her talk with Cole had calmed her overworked mind.

"No," she replied with a tired smile. "This is probably the last Christmas morning we'll get to sleep in for a long, long time. Let's embrace the ability to sleep while we still can." She tucked herself against Cole's chest, bringing her head to rest on his shoulder. "You're my favorite pillow," she said sleepily.

"I'm glad," he replied. Even as she faded into sleep, Abby could hear the smile in his voice and the gentle tug as he played with the ends of her hair.

Abby woke up to an empty bed and daylight peeking out from around the edges of the curtains. She reached over, feeling the spot where Cole normally slept. The sheets were room temperature, not warm like they usually were when he had recently vacated their bed. She sat up slowly, not wanting to make herself sick, and looked around the room, taking note of the time displayed on the clock that made its home on the nightstand next to her bed.

It was ten twenty-three. She'd gotten to sleep in one last Christmas morning, just like she had wanted to. She was only a little bit sad that her husband seemingly hadn't managed to do the same. Abby swung her legs down off the bed, and slid them into her warm, fuzzy slippers. She padded out of the bedroom and down the long hallway, following the gentle swell of Christmas music. A grin broke across Abby's face. Cole just couldn't help but get into the Christmas spirit; he'd been that way for as long as she'd known him. She imagined him one day in the not too distant future, dressing up as Santa as he passed out gifts to their children. Her hand rubbed over her stomach, and like Cole, she found herself getting impatient for the day when she'd be able to see the swell of her baby in her stomach, too. She imagined she might wish differently once her pants stopped fitting, but the new wardrobe would be worth it.

When Abby walked into the living room, she got the shock of her life. There were boxes and books *everywhere.* Unassembled cribs and bottles and stuffed animals were dangling precariously in random not-so-strategically-placed positions throughout the room. Even though she could hear Cole moving, he was nowhere to be found.

"Cole?" she said, her voice trembling a little. It was kind of like the entirety of several baby boutiques had vomited all over their living room.

He popped up out of the middle of a giant pile of boxes. "Hey," he said, at least having the decency to look a little embarrassed.

"What…Why…How…" She couldn't figure out exactly what it was she wanted to ask him. There were so many questions. *So* many. "It's Christmas morning, Cole. How did you even get all this?"

"We live in Manhattan. If you give someone your credit

card number, they'll bring you anything, anytime," he said with a guilty shrug.

"Did you leave a path so I could get to you?"

The worried look in Cole's eyes disappeared. "Over by the tree."

Abby made a beeline to the corner of the room, where there was a perfectly cleared path right into the mess of baby stuff Cole had purchased. When she reached him, she stood on her tiptoes and gave him a sweet good morning kiss.

"After you fell asleep, *I* couldn't sleep. I got on the computer, and the more I started reading the more overwhelmed I got, and I just *needed* to feel like I was in control of the situation, so I bought everything. Books and bottles and-"

"Cribs," Abby said. She couldn't hide the disappointment in her voice.

"Yeah."

"I wanted us to do that together. To pick out those things together."

She could practically hear Cole swallow as he wrapped her in his arms and kissed the top of her head. "I know. We'll give this stuff to people who really need it. I just lost my mind for a second."

Abby laughed, and looked around her. "Keep the books," she said, even though it seemed like he had purchased every single reading material on impending parenthood that was in existence, and there was no way they'd get through them all before the baby was born. "And that bear," she said, pointing to her right. "It's really cute."

Cole laughed. "I'm just…I'm really excited."

Abby kissed him then, letting her lips linger. "I know. Come here, I want to give you your present."

She and Cole had agreed to one big gift each. She could give him the framed sonogram card she wrapped yesterday, but he already knew she was pregnant, and his other gift would pack more of an emotional punch.

Cole followed Abby to the tree, and when she leaned down and plucked his gift from all the others, he did the same, retrieving a silvery envelope that piqued her curiosity.

Cole sat in Abby's favorite comfy chair, and pulled her onto his lap.

Abby handed him his present. "You first."

She was practically bursting at the seams with excitement. She'd been working on getting this gift for *months*, and there couldn't have been a more perfect time to give it to him.

Cole slid his fingers along the perfectly wrapped paper, admiring her handiwork. Slowly, he pulled on the edge of the bow until it unraveled, and then gently pulled the taped edges away from the paper, then placed both on the table beside them. The box rested on Abby's thighs, and her heart was pounding as Cole lifted the top.

His breath caught when he saw the book inside, and he carefully pulled it out of its wrapping. The slipcover was a little tattered, but was in fairly excellent shape.

"My dad used to read this to me when I was little," he whispered.

"I know," she replied, cupping his cheek. He had mentioned that he never was able to find that book in their library again, so she replaced it. "It's a first edition. I managed to get the author to sign it for you."

"You did?" Cole excitedly opened the front cover, reading the author's personalized inscription to him.

"It was truly a Christmas miracle. He's *really* old."

"Abby." Cole's voice was very soft. "Thank you."

She didn't know if it was the book that Cole loved or the fact that his father took some time out of his busy day to read it to him that made it so special, but Abby suspected it was a little bit of both.

"You're welcome." Abby took Cole's hand and brought it to her stomach. "You can read it to our baby now. It'll be like a Kerrigan family tradition."

There were tears shining in his eyes, and Abby couldn't help but kiss him.

"I love you," he breathed.

"I love *you*."

They sat in the quiet for a few minutes longer, the crackling of the fireplace the only sound in the room. Then Cole placed the silver envelope in Abby's hands. "Your turn."

She turned her head and grinned at him, sliding her finger under the envelope's flap and ripping it open. Inside was a brochure for an incredibly expensive and exclusive spa. "Fiji?" she asked, unable to hide her excitement.

"I thought you could use a little rest and relaxation. Although I bought this before I knew about the baby, and I'm not sure if we'll be able to go..."

"I'm sure it'll be okay, but we'll ask the doctor about it when we see her next week," she said, her voice almost an octave higher than usual.

Cole laughed, then kissed her shoulder. "Fair enough."

"You've always purchased real estate to commemorate our milestones, and I was worried you really *would* buy an island when I told you I was pregnant. A rented villa sounds like a nice compromise."

"I bought this before I found out about the baby. I still have time to buy the island."

Abby gave Cole a reproving look, but he just winked at her and smiled.

"We should call your parents," Abby said, sliding her hand along the fabric of Cole's shirt. "And then video chat Scott and Sara so the kids can see all the presents we have waiting for them under the tree."

"So they'll freak and start bugging Scott and Sara to bring them over now, now, *now*?"

Abby shrugged. "Yeah, that was kind of the idea."

Cole rubbed his stubbly chin along Abby's shoulder. "You have to be careful with that stuff now. We'll have some karmic retribution coming our way in a few years now."

"Yeah," Abby sighed, smiling. "That's true."

"Can we tell them?"

Abby wasn't quite ready to share the news yet; but she didn't want to voice exactly why. She wasn't naive; she knew it was still early, and so many things could happen, but she didn't want to bring him down. "Can we wait until after we see the doctor?"

"Yeah," Cole replied, and the gravity in his voice let Abby know that he knew exactly what she was worried about.

"That sounds like a good idea."

Abby placed her hand over where Cole's rested across her middle and gave it a squeeze. "When we're ready to tell everyone, we'll make a big thing out of it."

"Okay." Just like that, the smile was back in his voice. Abby loved that sound.

Abby turned toward the long wall of windows to their right, and noticed the snowflakes gently drifting through the sky. "Look!" she said, pointing.

Cole turned, and his face brightened. "Wow."

"C'mon." Abby hopped off of Cole's lap, then took his hand and walked him toward the french doors the led out to their balcony.

"Not so fast," he said, tugging on her hand to stop her momentum.

"What?"

"Coat," he said, his eyes drifting down to her stomach.

She rolled her eyes, but followed him over to the coat closet. Cole slipped his on, then helped Abby shrug into hers before wrapping her scarf around her neck. He pulled the lapels of her coat together and brought her in for a kiss before he led her outside.

They stood on the balcony, the newly fallen blanket of snow quieting the normally bustling city.

"Merry Christmas," Abby said, watching the snowflakes fluttering down from the pretty grey sky.

"Merry Christmas."

Then, unexpectedly, Cole dropped to his knees, parted her jacket and lifted up her shirt, then pressed his warm lips against her belly. "Merry Christmas to you, too," he said, giving her skin a soft caress.

Abby sighed as she ran her fingers through Cole's hair, wondering how she wasn't bursting apart from all the love and happiness she was feeling.

It was a indeed Merry Christmas, and she knew that they would have a lifetime more.

About the Author

Cassie Cross is a Maryland native and a romantic at heart, who lives outside of Baltimore with her two dogs and a closet full of shoes. Cassie's fondness for swoon-worthy men and strong women are the inspiration for most of her stories, and when she's not busy writing a book, you'll probably find her eating takeout and indulging in her love of 80's sitcoms.

Cassie loves hearing from her readers, so please follow her on Twitter (@ CrossWrites) or leave a review for this book on the site you purchased it from. Thank you!

Printed in Great Britain
by Amazon